DINOS DON'T
DO YOGA

Sounds True
Boulder, CO 80306

Published 2020

Book design by Karen Polaski

Printed in South Korea

Library of Congress Cataloging-in-Publication Data
Names: Bailey, Catherine (Children's story writer), author. | Willmore,
    Alex, illustrator.
Title: Dinos don't do yoga / by Catherine Bailey ; illustrations by Alex
    Willmore.
Other titles: Dinos do not do yoga
Description: Boulder, CO : Sounds True, 2020. | Audience: Ages 4-8. |
Identifiers: LCCN 2019056623 (print) | LCCN 2019056624 (ebook) | ISBN
    9781683644149 (hardcover) | ISBN 9781683644156 (ebook)
Subjects: CYAC: Dinosaurs--Fiction. | Yoga--Fiction. | Ability--Fiction.
Classification: LCC PZ7.1.B324 Din 2020 (print) | LCC PZ7.1.B324 (ebook)
    | DDC [E]--dc23
LC record available at https://lccn.loc.gov/2019056623
LC ebook record available at https://lccn.loc.gov/2019056624

10 9 8 7 6 5 4 3 2 1

DINOS DON'T DO YOGA

written by

CATHERINE BAILEY

illustrated by

ALEX WILLMORE

sounds true

BOULDER, COLORADO

This was Rex's valley.
And everything in Rex's valley was
roar-and-rumble rough
and talon-tearing TOUGH!

Even the plants.

That is, until Sam moved in.

Rex's ferocious friends could not decide if they liked the new dinosaur.

So Rex decided for them.

"Dinos don't do yoga."

"Dinos rage and stomp."

"Dinos are like ME.
Dinos chase and CHOMP!"

But Sam did not mind.
Instead he showed the ground sloths how to plank.

For some reason, this annoyed Rex even more.

"You'll never see a dino
wearing yoga pants."

"Standing on a mat,
mumbling silly chants."

Spinosaurus snickered. Allosaurus agreed.

And Iguanodon...paused.

"My neck is in knots, so I'd like to try,
maybe...just once...the butterfly."

Rex stormed off, and all his brutish buddies followed.

Well, not *all* of them.

Suddenly Rex realized he was alone.
And he didn't feel quite so tough anymore.

Then things went from bad to worse.

Betrayed and dismayed, Rex was so angry he couldn't see straight.

Which explains why he tripped over that bone...

and slid down that crater...

and rolled into that tar pit.

All the dinosaurs
rushed to help.

"Rex, buddy, are you okay?

We know you've had a rocky day."

Everyone started talking.

"I need to align my spines."

"These dino-thighs like exercise!"

"The biting, the brawling, the maiming, the mauling— it takes a toll!"

"Years of tussles
tore my muscles."

"I busted my back on that last attack."

Rex roared "THAT'S ENOUGH!"
Then he exhaled a teensy huff.

"I...I...
        I CAN'T do yoga! Not one pose.
I can't even...sniff...wipe my nose.

My jaws are deadly. My tail is spiny.
                My arms are strong!
        But also...tiny."

Sam stepped forward.
"It's okay. Don't feel blue.

Then the Yogasaur taught everyone

It's TOUGH to learn something new. Let's get you in your dino groove.
I think I know the perfect move."

the Tyrannosaurus...STRETCH!

All the dinos loved it, especially Rex.

"Listen Sam, I was wrong.
You did something very strong.

You were kind when I was rude.

And that makes you . . . one TOUGH dude."